T0353932

ALIEN SKY

DEBBIE VIALE

authorHOUSE®

AuthorHouse™
1663 Liberty Drive
Bloomington, IN 47403
www.authorhouse.com
Phone: 833-262-8899

Published by AuthorHouse 08/23/2021

ISBN: 978-1-6655-2481-0 (sc)
ISBN: 978-1-6655-2480-3 (e)

A boy was out in a large pasture with several cows grazing peacefully around him. The quiet setting became dark, and the wind started blowing. He saw a bright light approach from the sky.

As it got closer, he began to run along with the cattle. The boy hid behind a large tree trunk. This bright light landed in the distance in the large pasture.

The boy could see a craft that glowed in many colors, and it drew him out and away from the tree.

As it quietly glowed with its own language, the vibration was soothing and put him in a dreamlike state of mind. He didn't feel that he was in any danger.

The boy was startled by his cell phone ringing. It was his grandmother telling him it was time to come up to the house for dinner. He ran as fast as his legs could carry him. As he entered through the back door and sat down at the dinner table, he told his grandmother of his strange encounter while feeding the animals.

His grandmother went out with him to check on the animals, and everything seemed to be fine. So they finished their chores and went back inside.

Soon the dogs started barking. The boy grabbed two flashlights and said, "Let's go out to the barnyard to see what's upsetting the dogs. That thing I saw might be back." His grandmother went out with him. They could feel a strong vibration and see a bright light coming from the large pasture behind the barn.

The glow and vibration seemed to be soothing, and they didn't feel they were in any danger.

As a glowing, fluid-type door opened on a craft behind the lights, out stepped a strange, small man with large black eyes, a small mouth, and a small nose.

There were three other humanoids inside the craft.

The boy and his grandmother were asked to enter the craft and told they were not in any danger.

However, they were told that they were in danger of losing the human race as they knew it. The aliens asked the grandmother if she would go with them to talk to scientists and help convince them to work on a new vaccine to save lives. Otherwise, humans would be in danger of losing many lives here on Earth due to an out-of-control virus. She asked, "Why me?"

One of the aliens replied, "Because you are a scientist and that's what it's going to take to make them listen to your cries for help."

They explained she would be safe, along with her grandson, and not gone long because their craft would go back in history and forward to the future but their time would stand still until they returned. That object continued to glow.

With the grandmother and her grandson inside, it took off at a rapid speed and then disappeared.

It slowly landed at a facility where scientists were in white jumpsuits inside a white van and awaiting them.

They were taken to a building with a large science lab where their DNA was harvested. The woman's DNA and an alien man's DNA were combined as they worked on finding a vaccine to cure this out-of-control virus. Scientists explained that crossing alien DNA with human DNA would cause molecular structures to become mutated within the gene pool. These mutations then could be cloned into many cells and colonized to activate a much faster healing process.

Adjusting hormone levels with oxytocin spikes put the healing process into overdrive. The grandmother and grandson were asked many questions and then told to visit 2023 to find out if this virus was known to kill many people.

Then back to 2001 before returning to 2020, where they were able to warn many scientists and work closely with NASA to eradicate any future outbreaks. They found this virus had been eradicated due to a vaccine that was created in 2019. It had been used in trials with promising results with a short-lived pandemic in 2020 with a shelter-in-place order that had been lifted as people filled the streets again.

This changed the outlook of many people, and they came together as a nation once more, not knowing what could have destroyed them in their future.

As they landed safely at the ranch, the woman couldn't stop thinking the same thoughts the alien man was thinking as she would think of an answer back to him. Her thought process was changed into a mental communication between the two.

Once she and her grandson were home safe, knowing she had gone to three different eras in time, she felt compelled to thank this alien man and trustingly gave him a kiss on the cheek.

He looked surprised as a tear fell from his eye down his cheek. He didn't know what it was.

As she wiped away his tear from where she had kissed him, he explained they never shed tears where he came from.

She smiled politely and replied, "Welcome to my world, where we survive through our strength and love."

Printed in the United States
by Baker & Taylor Publisher Services